I Know the River Loves Me

Yo sé que el río me ama

Maya Christina Gonzalez

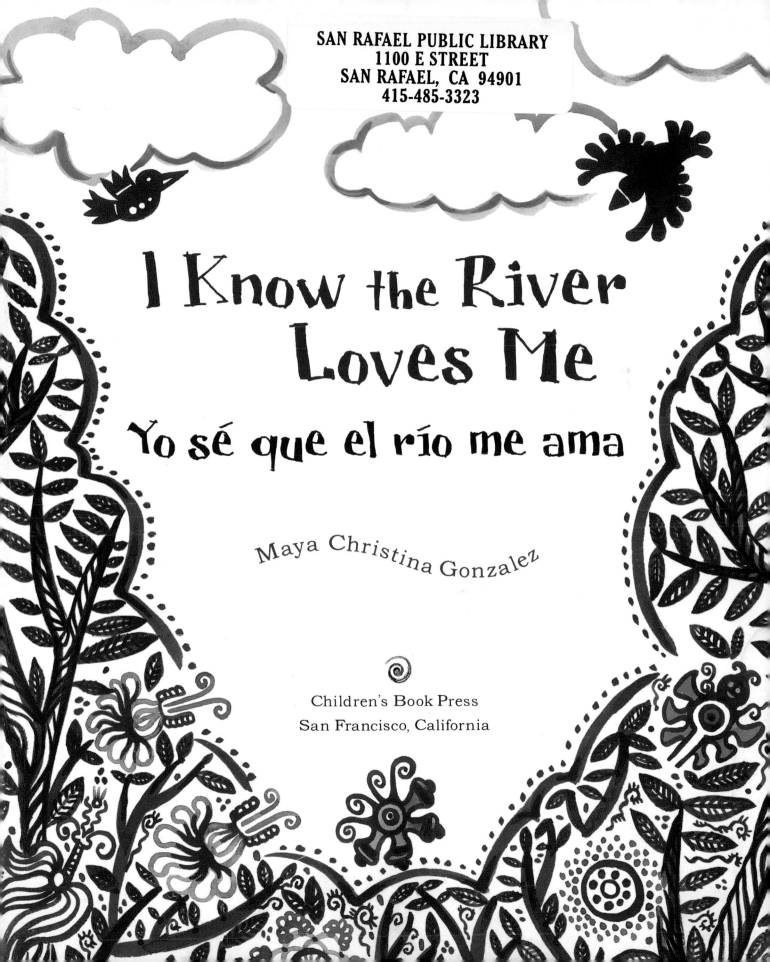

Children's Book Press
San Francisco, California

I am here to visit one of
my best friends in the world—
the river. She loves me.

Estoy aquí para visitar con uno
de mis mejores amigos en el mundo:
el río. El río me ama.

I know the river loves me because I can
hear her calling me as soon as I am close.

Yo sé que el río me ama porque tan pronto
como me acerco oigo que me llama.

She jumps and sings when she sees me.

Cuando me ve, salta y canta.

I run to her side and she cools me down.

8

Corro a su lado

y me refresca.

I know the river loves me because when
I look into her face, she's happy to see me.

Yo sé que el río me ama porque cuando
lo miro a la cara, está contento de verme.

When I jump on
her back she holds
me up. When I leap
into her arms she takes
me in.

Cuando brinco sobre
su espalda, me sostiene.
Cuando salto a sus
brazos, me acoge.

12

She tugs on my hair and my arms
and we flow together.

Me acaricia el pelo y los brazos
y fluimos juntos.

I watch her change like me.
In the winter, she is low and quiet.
In the summer,
she is full and loud.

Veo que el río cambia como cambio yo.
En el invierno, está bajo y tranquilo.
En el verano, está lleno y ruidoso.

17

The river takes care of me and I take care of the river.
I only leave behind what already belongs to her.

El río me cuida y yo cuido al río.
Sólo dejo atrás lo que ya a él le pertenece.

I know the river loves me.
The next time I come she will be here
waiting for me, singing my name.

Yo sé que el río me ama porque cuando
yo regrese a visitarlo, él me estará esperando,
cantando mi nombre.

20

I know the river loves me,
and I love the river.

Yo sé que el río me ama,
y yo amo al río.

Photos by Matthew Smith-Gonzalez

My love of rivers began when I was a child

camping across California and Oregon. As a grown-up I sought out rivers around the world. I floated down the Ganges River in India. I sat at the foot of a waterfall in the Puerto Rican rainforest. I rested beside the river in Maua, Brazil and warmed myself in the hot waters of a spring in Oaxaca, Mexico. I have spent time with more rivers than I can count, all of whom I have loved and could feel them love me.

But no river has touched my heart the way the Yuba River in California has. I tell my daughter that we are "river people", here to learn how to flow with all of life, and to let life flow through us. I have gone to the Yuba for many years now. She is a part of me. She's family. Everyone can visit her at the South Yuba Independence Trail, the country's first wheelchair accessible trail. You can learn more about her at:

www.sequoyachallenge.org

Love,
Maya

Maya Christina Gonzalez

is a river lover. Although she has visited rivers the world over, her favorite river is the Yuba in California. She is an acclaimed fine artist, educator and award-winning children's book illustrator. She has created artwork for 20 children's books. This is the second book that she has both written and illustrated. Maya lives, paints and plays in San Francisco, California.

I dedicate this book to my husband Matthew, my daughter Zai Velvet, and to the rivers of the world, all of whom teach me to open wider and let life and love flow through me with greater and greater strength. Thank you for every moment! —MCG

Story and illustrations copyright © 2009 by Maya Christina Gonzalez
Publisher/Executive Director: Lorraine Garcia-Nakata
Executive Editor / Art Direction & Design: Dana Goldberg
Thanks to Laura Chastain, Ina Cumpiano, Teresa Mlawer, and
the staff of Children's Book Press: Janet, Rod, Christina, and Imelda.

Library of Congress Cataloging-in Publication Data
Gonzalez, Maya Christina.
 I know the river loves me / story and pictures, Maya Christina Gonzalez
 Yo sé que el río me ama / cuento e ilustraciones, Maya Christina Gonzalez.
  p. cm.
 Summary: A girl expresses her love of the river that she visits, plays in, and cares for throughout the year.
 ISBN-13: 978-0-89239-233-9 (hardcover)
 ISBN-10: 0-89239-233-9 (hardcover)
 1. Rivers—Fiction. 2. Spanish language materials—Bilingual. I. Title.
II. Title: Yo sé que el río me ama.
 PZ73.G5888 2009
 E—dc22   2008053194

Children's Book Press is a 501(c)(3)
non-profit organization. Our work is made possible in part by the following contributors: AT&T Foundation, John Crew and Sheila Gadsden, The San Francisco Foundation, The San Francisco Arts Commission, National Endowment for the Arts, Carlota del Portillo, Union Bank of California, the Children's Book Press Board of Directors, and the Anonymous Fund of the Greater Houston Community Foundation. For a catalog, write: Children's Book Press, 965 Mission Street, Suite 425, San Francisco, California, 94103. Visit us on the web at: www.childrensbookpress.org

Printed in Malaysia by Tien Wah Press.
10 9 8 7 6 5 4 3 2 1
Contact the publisher for sales information. Quantity discounts available for educational or nonprofit use.